A SKY FULL OF KITES

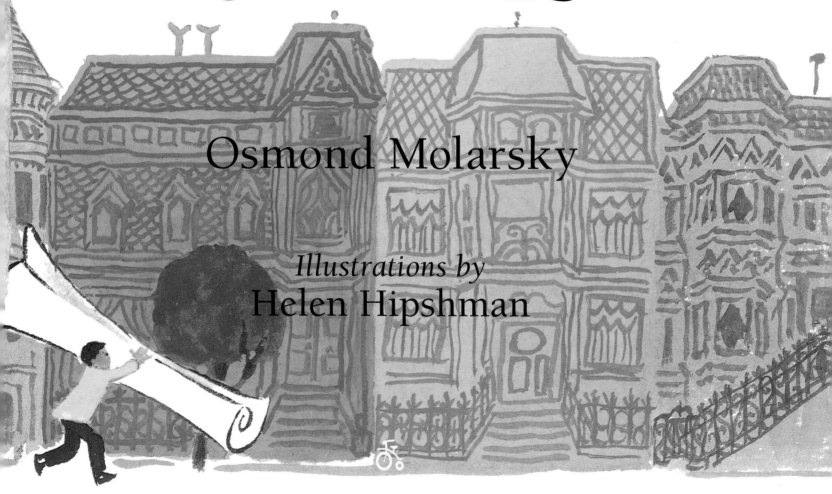

Osmond Molarsky

Illustrations by
Helen Hipshman

TRICYCLE PRESS
Berkeley, California

TRICYCLE PRESS
P.O. Box 7123
Berkeley, California 94707

Cover and text design by Helen Hipshman

Library of Congress Cataloging-in-Publication Data

Molarsky, Osmond.
    A sky full of kites / Osmond Molarsky ; illustrations, Helen Hipshman.
        p. cm.
    Summary: Young Colin, a Chinese American boy in San Francisco, shows determination and ingenuity
in finding a way to exhibit his art.
    ISBN 1-883672-26-0
    [1. Artists—Fiction. 2. Kites—Fiction. 3. San Francisco (Calif.)—Fiction. 4. Chinese Americans—Fiction.]
    I. Hipshman, Helen D., ill.   II. Title
    PZ7.M7317Sk 1996
    [E]—dc20   94-49535
                                                                                                    CIP
                                                                                                    AC

First Tricycle Press printing, 1996
Manufactured in Singapore

1 2 3 4 5 6 — 01 00 99 98 97 96

To Marina

—O.M.

To Adam

—H.H.

From the very first, Colin liked to draw.

As he grew older…

…he just drew all the time.

The first thing Colin wanted to do when he got some new paints was paint a gigantic picture.

"Not on the wall, Colin!" his mother said. "Let me show you what you can do."

She showed him how to glue together large sheets of paper, and soon Colin was painting a fantastic, gigantic picture. He was so excited, he wanted to show it to everybody.

So he rolled the picture up
and took it to school.

"Very nice," said his teacher. "But if I put up your picture, there won't be enough room to put up pictures by other children. I'm sorry."

Colin was disappointed, but he did not give up. "The firehouse!" he thought.

The firehouse had a big front door. The perfect place to show his painting.

"Sorry," said the chief. "It's against firehouse rules and regulations."
Colin was disappointed, but he did not give up. How about the Grand
Emporium?

"Glad to take a look at your painting," said the manager of the Grand Emporium. "Please unroll it. Hmmm. I see. Afraid we can't have pictures of monsters in this store. They would frighten the children. Sorry."

"That's silly," thought Colin. "Children love monsters." Colin was disappointed, but he did not give up. "The bank!"

Colin went straight to the First National Bank. Inside, he saw a perfect place to put his painting. "Oh, I'm afraid not," said the vice president. "That place is reserved for the picture of Homer B. Humbolt, founder and first president of First National. It's out of the question to put your picture up there."

Colin left the bank disappointed, but he did not give up.

He was marching along, still hoping to find a place where everyone would see his picture, when he saw a church.

"What a beautiful painting," said the minister. "But come inside, please."

Colin looked around him. In the whole tremendous church, there were no walls, only windows—each a beautiful picture with the sunlight shining through it. "I understand," said Colin. "Thank you." And he went on his way. Colin was disappointed, but he did not give up. He already was thinking of the freight yard.

"Can I put my picture on the side of your boxcar?" he asked the brakeman.
"Do you know who will see it up there?" the brakeman asked.
"Who?" asked Colin.

“Cows,” the brakeman replied. “The freight train runs mostly through woods and fields.”

“Cows!” said Colin. “No, thank you,” and he moved on. Colin was disappointed. There *had* to be a place to show his picture.

When he got to the art museum, Colin thought, "Of course. This is it."

"Beautiful!" said the curator. "We'll hang your picture on our grandest wall."

"I'll help you," said Colin, and got out a roll of tape and some thumbtacks.

"Not so fast, young man, we can't put up your picture until next year. There's a waiting list."

"Next year! That's much too long!" Colin thought, and he took his picture away. He wandered off to the park beside the bay. There, some children were flying kites.

Colin had a fantastic idea. He rushed home and turned his monster painting into a huge, huge kite.

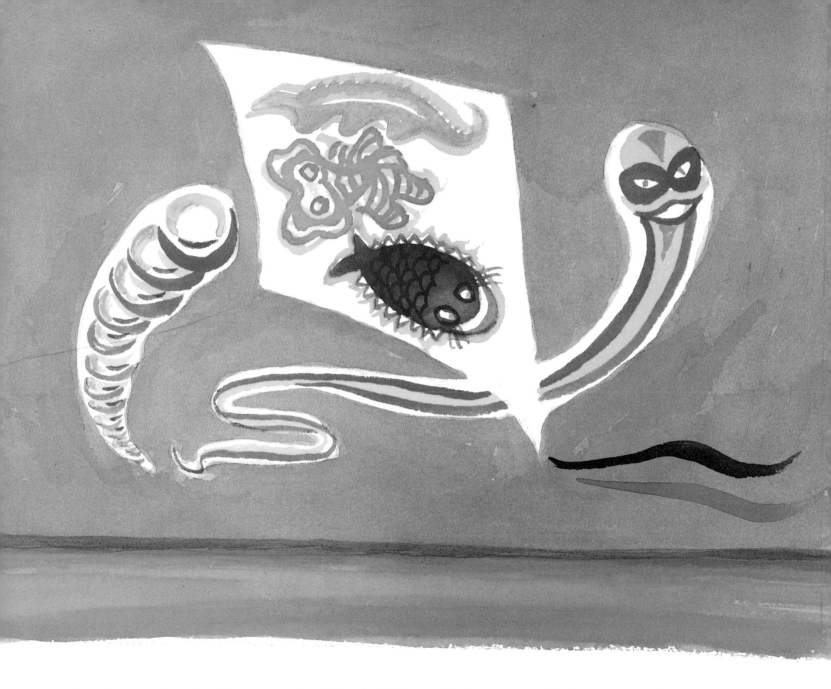

In the park, the kite nearly lifted Colin off the ground, but some boys
pulled him down and helped him hold it. Then, after a while, they tied it to
a tree, and it flew by itself.

Colin's kite stayed up in the sky for three days and three nights, and crowds of people saw it. Everyone talked about the huge kite with the monster pictures on it. The newspaper showed it on the front page, and of course it was on the television news, up high beside the moon. Colin had to stand before the television camera and answer a few questions. This made him well known all over the city.

The very next week, the art museum found room for Colin's painting, but the vice president of the First National Bank, the manager of the Grand Emporium, and the fire chief had to wait their turns.

Best of all, Colin's mother let him put his next painting up on the living room wall and leave it there just as long as he liked.